ALBERT'S PLAY
by Leslie Tryon

ATHENEUM   1992   NEW YORK

MAXWELL MACMILLAN CANADA
Toronto

MAXWELL MACMILLAN INTERNATIONAL
New York   Oxford   Singapore   Sydney

Special thanks to Con Pederson.

Atheneum
Macmillan Publishing Company
866 Third Avenue
New York, NY 10022

Maxwell Macmillan Canada, Inc.
1200 Eglinton Avenue East
Suite 200
Don Mills, Ontario M3C 3N1

Macmillan Publishing Company is part of the Maxwell
Communication Group of Companies.

First edition
Printed in Hong Kong by South China Printing Company (1988) Ltd.
10 9 8 7 6 5 4 3 2 1
The text of this book is set in 14 pt. Bookman Light.
The illustrations are rendered in watercolors and colored pencils.

Library of Congress Cataloging-in-Publication Data
Tryon, Leslie.
Albert's play/by Leslie Tryon. —1st ed.
p.   cm.
Summary: Albert helps the children of Pleasant Valley School stage
a play.
ISBN 0-689-31525-2
[1. Theater—Production and direction—Fiction.   2. Geese—Fiction.
3. Stories in rhyme.]   I. Title.
PZ8.3.T77A1   1992
[E]—dc20   91-23145

For Norma
and
for Art,
with love
  —L. T.

It's time for that yearly tradition,
  The production of Albert's play.
Will children who wish to audition
  Be on stage after school today!

As soon as Albert had picked out the cast,
    He set the crew into motion.
They began with a tub and a flagpole mast,
    And they painted the blue of the ocean.
The stars, the moon, the bongs, and the boat—
    There were too many things to do!
Posters to draw, and boxes to tote,
    And learning to dance on cue,
        On cue,
        On cue,
    And learning to dance on cue.

They dangled the stars and the dancing moon
    While working faster and faster.
No one had yet found a runcible spoon—
    This could be a disaster!
There were masks to make too, to cut, and to glue.
    Would they ever get everything done?
Rehearsal was called for half-past two.
    Who said doing a play would be fun,
        Be fun,
        Be fun?
    Who said doing a play would be fun?

Albert fixed the lights and wiped some tears.
  They rehearsed until it was right.
He soothed those last-minute jitters and fears,
  And said, "You'll be fine by tonight."
They put on their costumes, practiced a bow,
  Albert double-checked every detail.
The theater is full—*Shhhh! it's just minutes now,*
  Till the Owl and the Pussy-cat sail,
    Set sail,
    Set sail,
  Till the Owl and the Pussy-cat sail.

Ladies and Gentleman...

The Owl and the Pussy-cat
by Edward Lear

The Owl and the Pussy-cat went to sea
    In a beautiful pea-green boat,
They took some honey, and plenty of money,
    Wrapped up in a five-pound note.
The Owl looked up to the stars above,
    And sang to a small guitar,
'O lovely Pussy! O Pussy, my love,
    What a beautiful Pussy you are,
        You are,
        You are!
    What a beautiful Pussy you are!'

Pussy said to the Owl, 'You elegant fowl!
    How charmingly sweet you sing!
O let us be married! Too long we have tarried:
    But what shall we do for a ring?'
They sailed away, for a year and a day,
    To the land where the Bong-tree grows
And there in a wood a Piggy-wig stood
    With a ring at the end of his nose,
        His nose,
        His nose,
    With a ring at the end of his nose.

'Dear Pig, are you willing to sell for one shilling
Your ring?' Said the Piggy, 'I will.'

So they took it away, and were married next day
By the Turkey who lives on the hill.

They dined on mince, and slices of quince,
 Which they ate with a runcible spoon;
And hand in hand, on the edge of the sand,
 They danced by the light of the moon,
  The moon,
  The moon,
 They danced by the light of the moon.